Brutus is a Champion!

Written by Melissa Lee Wright

Illustrated by Skylar Howe

Copyright©2019 by Melissa Lee Wright
All rights reserved. No part of this book may be reproduced or transmitted in any form or by any means without written permission from the author.
Printed in the United States
ISBN-13: 978-1-68778-665-4

Adam,
   Always believe in yourself!
            — Melissa Lee Wright

Brutus

Dedication

I dedicate this book to Erron Wright Jr, the biggest dreamer I've ever known. He dreamed of having a pet pig as a little boy, just as I did as a little girl. Without him, I wouldn't have had the adventure of knowing a little pig named Brutus.
For that I will be forever thankful.

Brutus jumped out of bed! Today was the day! He was finally going to get his blue belt in karate class tonight! He had worked so hard and waited so long and it was finally here!

Karate (*kuh-rah-tee*) a Japanese art of self-defense in which you use your hands and feet.

That evening when Mommy walked Brutus into the Dojo, everyone was dressed in their gis and were getting ready for class to start. Brutus put his gi on, tied his orange belt, and lined up with the other students.

Dojo (*doh-jo*) a school for teaching karate.

They all bowed in to Sensei Goo and class began. All of the white, yellow and orange belts were working together in a group. Brutus couldn't help watching what all of the blue belts were doing in their group. He was so excited to join them, but he was a little sad. He was going to miss his beginner group.

Sensei (*sen-say*) a teacher of karate.

They had been with him for all he had learned so far! He learned kata and kumite and had gone to many competitions with this group.

They were friends and cheered each other on. What was he going to do without them?

Kata *(kaw-ta)* movements made by karate students.

Kumite *(koo-muh-tay)* fighting in a friendly competition.

At the end of class Sensei Goo called Brutus to the front of the class and presented him with his blue belt. Sensei had Brutus bow to him and then the whole class bowed to Brutus!
Mommy was so proud of him!
She said, "You're my little champion."
Brutus just smiled.

A couple of weeks went by and Brutus was fitting right in with the blue belt group. They were nice, but a little bigger and older. He missed his friends, but had worked too hard to turn back! His big tournament was this weekend. He was going to be ready for it… he hoped.

Tournament (*turn-a-mint*) a contest of skill and courage between competitors.

The night before the tournament Mommy and Daddy said a special prayer for Brutus at bedtime. It made him feel better and he wasn't as nervous. He knew with God on his side that he could do anything!

I can do everything through Christ who gives me strength.
Philippians 4:13

The next day at the tournament
Brutus won 1ˢᵗ place in kata!
His trophy was bigger than he was!

It was now time for his big fight. He did what
Sensei Goo taught him in class and he won
5 points to 2 points! He looked around and
all of his friends were there cheering him on!
They said, "Brutus, we knew you were a Champion!"

Whatever you do, do everything for the glory of God.
1 Corinthians 10:31

Characters

Brutus - Little Pig

Goo - Liger

Avery - Monkey

Jackson - Little Liger

Erron Sr. - Lion

Betty - Tiger

Pablo - Porcupine

Nate - Dog

Duke - Giraffe

Richard Jr. - Eagle

Jakob - Rhino

Emma - Skunk

ABOUT THE AUTHOR

Hi, I'm Melissa Lee Wright. Born and raised in Southwest Missouri, I'm a busy Christian wife, Momma of five kiddos, and a Health Insurance Agent by day. In addition, I'm very active in my community, love art, traveling, reading, cooking and sports. Though I never really saw myself as an author, I'm so happy the Lord gave me Brutus and the inspiration to write about our adventures!

ABOUT THE ILLUSTRATOR

Skylar Howe is from Granby, Missouri. She is currently enrolled in the Early Childhood Education program at Missouri State University. She has always had a passion for creating and hopes to one day become an art teacher.

Brutus Lee Wright

Made in the USA
Columbia, SC
02 March 2020